New Kid
on
Spurwink
Ave.

New Kid on Spurwink Ave.

Michael Crowley

Illustrated by Abby Carter

Little, Brown and Company
Boston Toronto London

Text copyright © 1992 by Michael Crowley
Illustrations copyright © 1992 by Abby Carter

First Edition

Library of Congress Cataloging-in-Publication Data

Crowley, Michael.
   New kid on Spurwink Ave. / Michael Crowley; illustrated by
Abby Carter. — 1st ed.
     p. cm.
   Summary: The new kid in the neighborhood resists the attempts
of the Spurwink Gang to involve him in their activities, until finally
he is ready to unveil his amazing invention.
   ISBN 0-316-16230-2
   [1. Neighborliness — Fiction. 2. Inventions — Fiction.]
I. Carter, Abby, ill. II. Title. III. Title: New kid on Spurwink Ave.
PZ7.C8876Ne 1992
[E] — dc20   90-39064

10 9 8 7 6 5 4 3 2 1

WOR

Published simultaneously in Canada
by Little, Brown and Company (Canada) Limited

Printed in the United States of America

For Kathryn Yates, Michael and Maggie
And just remember one thing...

M.C.

For Doug

A.C.

When Leonard moved into Corey Budd's old house, right away our mom said, "Why don't you invite him into your little club?"

"It's not a 'little club,' Mom." We must have told her
a million times. "We're the Spurwink Gang."
"Yes, well, *gang* sounds a bit fierce, don't you think?"

"We *are* fierce. And what if Leonard is boring or something? Not everybody gets in, you know."
"At least invite him over to play," she said.

So we did.

We said, "Leonard, want to come up and see
Dark Mountain?" We took him up over Old Clothes
Ridge . . . across Trap Door Swamp . . . through
Fly Bat Alley . . . to Dark Mountain!

And Leonard said, "Naw, man, it's just some old boxes
in the attic."

But he showed up the next day. So we said, "Leonard, want to play Sword Pirates?" And we got our swords and shields and headed out to Rummy Sea. "Ahoy! Skull and bones dead ahead! Full rudder the main jib, mates! Long John Leonard, be smart with yer sword!"

"Naw, man," Leonard said, "it's just a puny stick."

And there he was again that afternoon. "Leonard, want to play Round Up?" "Saddle up!" "Yip-ee-ii-ooo!" "Let's ride!" "Round up that straggler, Len. Lasso that ol' steer!"

"Naw, man, it's just the dumb dog."

That night, Mom said, "How's it going with Leonard?"
"Boringboringboring. He never wants to do anything."
"Maybe he's shy," she said. "Have you tried to find out
what he's interested in?"
"Who cares? Nobody wants him in the Spurwink Gang."
Mom raised one of her eyebrows, the serious one.

So the next day we said, "Leonard, want to play Hurricane?"
And we put on our foul-weather gear and hunched out into
the storm. Rain whipped our faces. Thunder boomed all
around. "She's a bad one. Better check the dam, it could go
any minute! Ever seen anything like this rain, Lenny?"

"Naw, man, it's just the garden hose."

And when we said, "Leonard, want to play Circus? Ladies and Gentlemen, from the jungles of Kyroba, the world's greatest lion tamer, Leo! nardo! Watch him laugh in the face of danger. See him place his entire head inside the jaws of the fiercest creatures on earth!" — he said:

"Naw, man, it's just a coupla stuffed animals."

"Leonard," we said, "is that your mom calling you?"

"Say," he said, "want to come over to my house tomorrow?"

"Ah, well, gee . . . we're going to be kind of busy. . . ."

"Oh," he said. "OK."

That night we told Mom, "We've tried everything!"

"It takes time to make friends," she said.

"This guy could take forever! Or worse, all summer vacation!"

"Whew," we said, and the next day we got the whole
Spurwink Gang together for some fun.
"Hey, where's Naw Man?" somebody asked. "Shhhhhh!"
we said.   "Let's head for Kettle Cove before he finds us."

But just then came a sudden, tremendous buzzing and whirring and clanking. It grew louder and louder. "It's a motorcycle!" someone yelled. "No! It's a tank! It's, it's — it's coming right down Spurwink Ave.!"

And before we could move, the strangest, loudest, and possibly coolest vehicle we ever saw came rumbling down the sidewalk right past us. It pulled a U-turn in Big Liza's driveway, honked, and zoomed by the other way.

The entire Spurwink Gang was stunned. Finally someone said: "Was that Leonard?"

We hopped on our bikes and pedaled full speed over to
Corey Budd's old house. Sure enough, there was Leonard.
There was the vehicle. And there in his garage was a whole
collection of gizmos, contraptions, and wild stuff like nobody
had ever seen.

"Leonard," we said, "this is amazing. Did your parents buy this stuff for you?"

"Naw, man." He smiled. "I built it."

"All this?"

"Yeah. That's what I like to do, build things. Want to see how some of this stuff works?"

We spent the rest of the day riding around and playing with everything, while Leonard grinned and messed around with his tools. And just yesterday we thought he was boring!

"Naw Man," we said, "you're a genius."
And it just so happened the Spurwink Gang had an opening
for a genius builder.